THE
FOREST
CHILD

THE FOREST CHILD

Richard Edwards
Illustrated by Peter Malone

Orchard Books
New York

To Helen, for her patience
P.M.

Text copyright © 1995 by Richard Edwards
Illustrations copyright © 1995 by Peter Malone
First American Edition 1995 published by Orchard Books
First published in Great Britain by Orion Children's Books in 1995

Orchard Books
95 Madison Avenue
New York, NY 10016

Manufactured in Italy
Book design by Tracey Cunnell

10 9 8 7 6 5 4 3 2 1

Library of Congress Cataloging-in-Publication Data
Edwards, Richard, date.
The forest child / Richard Edwards ; illustrated by Peter Malone.
— 1st American ed.   p.   cm.
Summary: A boy from the nearby village befriends a girl who has been
raised by the animals of the forest and later helps rescue her from a hunter.
ISBN 0-531-09463-4
[1. Feral children—Fiction.   2. Forest animals—Fiction.]
I. Malone, Peter, date, ill.   II. Title.
PZ7.E26385Fo   1995   [E]—dc20   94-45800

There was once a child who was
raised by the animals of the forest.

The wolf taught her to run.

The bear taught her to find food.

The beaver taught her to swim.

She ran silently over the forest floor.
She knew where to find honey and the juiciest berries.

She dived in the lake behind the beaver dam.

One day a hunter came to the forest, bringing with
him a boy from the village to carry his traps and snares.
"Stay here and don't move till I get back!" said the hunter.

But the boy got bored sitting still. He walked between the trees,
where the light was dim. It was like being under water in a green sea.

At the edge of a clearing, the boy from the village met the forest child.

She backed away, growling like a wolf.

"Who are you?" called the boy. "Don't be afraid."

But the girl turned and ran off into the shadows.

The boy wanted to see her again. Each day that followed, the boy returned to the clearing, hoping to meet the forest child once more.

At last, she lost all fear of him and they would walk together
along twisting paths in the forest's secret heart.

One day the hunter was out checking his traps and saw the children passing.
He followed them back to the clearing. When the boy had left for home,
the hunter burst from his hiding place and grabbed the forest child.
"Caught you, little bird!" he snarled.

The hunter took the wild girl to the village. She fought and bit and twisted
and kicked, but the hunter was too strong for her. He locked her up.

The hunter decided to teach the girl how to behave. He gave her a cup to drink from and a spoon to eat with, but she didn't know what they were for.

The girl would not speak, so the hunter laid a sheet of paper on the table.
"Here, write your name," he said, giving her a pen.

The girl looked at the pen and turned it over in her hand.

She didn't understand what she was supposed to do.

"What's the matter with you?" shouted the hunter.

The girl's eyes glittered with tears. She wanted to go back to the forest.

"WRITE YOUR NAME!"
The girl stood up. She broke the pen in pieces and
threw them at the hunter, spattering him with ink.
"You stupid girl!" he yelled, raising his arm.

Just then the village boy hammered on the door.
"Don't shout at her," he said.
"She doesn't understand."

"She'd better understand soon," said the hunter, "or there'll be trouble!
And there'll be trouble for you too, if you don't mind your own business!"
He slammed the door.

The boy hesitated for a moment and then turned towards the forest.

The animals of the forest missed the girl they had raised.

All day they ran between the tall trees, searching. They found her scent on the ground and followed it to the clearing, where it mixed with other scents.

The wolf howled.

On the outskirts of the village, the animals met the boy coming to find them.
"Quick! This way!"

The animals leapt in through the windows.

They chased the hunter around the room,
out into the darkness, and across the fields.

The wolf bit a hole in the hunter's trousers, the beaver tripped him,
and the bear sent him rolling down a hill,

right into the middle of a big mud puddle.
The hunter sank from sight.

The sun streams down like gold between the trees.
The girl and the village boy run silently over the forest floor.

She teaches him to find honey and the juiciest berries.
They swim and dive in the lake behind the beaver dam.

They all sleep together in a jumbled heap,
under a million stars.